The Beautiful Princess Without a Face

Written by April Robins, F. Jay Robins and Celeste Robins

AuthorHouse™
1663 Liberty Drive, Suite 200
Bloomington, IN 47403
www.authorhouse.com
Phone: 1-800-839-8640

First published by AuthorHouse 10/29/2007

ISBN: 978-1-4343-3801-3 (sc)

Library of Congress Control Number: 2007908447

Printed in the United States of America
Bloomington, Indiana

This book is printed on acid-free paper.

authorHOUSE®

Other stories by April Robins

A Message of Love
Fisher Lives on a River
Where is My Bennie?
Wolfie of Robin Falls
Zachary Goes Treasure Hunting

Available for purchase through www.authorhouse.com,
or by calling 1-888-280-7715.

With loving admiration to our beautiful Princess,
Sarah.

Also with love to our:
Austin, Eli, & Zachary

Wishing you the loveliest of daydreams!

Sarah pulled her soft, fuzzy robe close to her body. It felt so warm. It worked as a napkin when no one was looking.

In the kitchen, the smell of breakfast filled the air. "I want another piece of bacon and a donut," she said.

Sarah loved to taste the powdered sugar and watch it fall off onto her clothes. She made believe that it was snowflakes.

"No problem, Little Princess," her Daddy replied.

Soon, Daddy must come up with a new title for Sarah. She was growing up. She was not going to be little much longer.

Sarah was tall and slim for her age, like a model. She was kind to everyone. Her family and friends adored her.

As most girls do, Sarah had reached the age of self-doubt. Her front teeth were growing back, and she started to wonder if she was beautiful or just pretty.

Sarah was holding her new doll when she returned to the family room. Her grandmother gave her this antique, china doll for Christmas.

It was New Year's morning. Everyone was still in their nightclothes watching their new, big screen TV.

"Oh, the parade is on the TV!" Sarah exclaimed.

Sarah could see a colorful float with a beautiful, young lady sitting on top. Sarah believed the beauty queen was waving at her.

Sarah stretched out on the sofa. She was hugging her new doll.

Soon, Sarah drifted off into a dreamlike state. In her daydream, she became her beautiful Indian Princess China doll. Everyone called her Princess-Loves-the-Pond.

She lived in Doll Land across the moonbeams.

She was tall and slim. She wore Native American clothes with bright and shiny beads.

Princess-Loves-the-Pond had the beauty of a Princess. On the other hand, her deeds were not quite as nice.

Her father was the leader of her doll tribe. Her mother helped the women in the tribe who were in need.

Her mother asked Princess-Loves-the-Pond to taste the soup she was cooking for a sick friend. Her mother needed to know if it was salty enough.

Princess-Loves-the-Pond thought she was too beautiful to be a food taster. Her taste buds should be reserved for the finer foods in life.

Lucy, the rubber doll, made candles for the doll tribe. She loved to add sweet fragrances to her candles. She asked Princess-Loves-the-Pond to smell her wax and give her approval.

Princess-Loves-the-Pond thought she was too beautiful for that sweaty job. She worried that her long, silky hair might fall into the pot of hot wax. It would take her days to comb out the wax.

Richie, the rag doll, was a member of the tribal band. He played the water drum and wanted Princess-Loves-the-Pond to hear them rehearse. He asked her to sing with the band. After all, she had a lovely voice.

Princess-Love-the-Pond did not want to listen to all that noise. It might hurt her eardrums. She had perfect pitch. Why waste her talent.

Princess-Loves-the-Pond admired herself daily. She went into the woods to see her reflection in the pond.

The wild animals stayed nearby. They longed for the beautiful Princess to notice them. Princess-Love-the-Pond seldom saw those magnificent creatures.

She only found time to see herself.

Princess-Loves-the-Pond always asked the pond, "Am I beautiful?"

The pond always replied, "Yes, my Princess."

One day Princess-Loves-the-Pond bent over to see her reflection. She slipped on a stone and fell into the pond. A gush of water washed away her delicate face.

She no longer had eyes, ears, nose, or a mouth.

Princess-Loves-the-Pond could no longer use four of her five senses.

She could no longer *see*, *hear*, *taste*, or *smell*. She could only *feel*. It was not long before she realized the value of what she lost.

She was lucky that her pet wolf was in the forest. He led her safely home.

Princess-Loves-the-Pond loved the *feel* of the:

Rough bumps on stones

Touch of her father's hand

Soft, silky fur of her pet wolf

Grains of sand between her toes

Arms of friends extended at a pow-wow

At least, she could still *feel.*

Princess-Loves-the-Pond longed once again to *see*:

Bright colors of wildflowers

The love in her mother's eyes

Waves crashing against the rocks

Movement of wild animals in the forest

Stars sparkling at night alongside the glow of the moon

Princess-Loves-the-Pond desired once again to *hear:*

A bubbling brook

Crackling of a fire

Howling of her pet wolf

Hooting of the owl at night

Laughter from around the campfire

Richie's band playing at the ceremonies

Princess-Loves-the-Pond dreamed once again of using her mouth to *taste:*

Sweet honey licked off her fingers

The salty flavor of her mother's soup

Tart wild berries picked from the field

Morning porridge made from hominy grits

Roasted turkey so tender it falls from the drumstick

Frybread prepared by her mother using a family recipe

Princess-Loves-the-Pond yearned once again to *smell* the:

Fragrance of pine trees

Aroma of dinner cooking

Scent of rain as it hit the grass

Sweetness of her friend's candles burning

Perfume of springtime flowers, especially the honeysuckle

Several full moons had passed since Princess-Loves-the-Pond last saw her reflection. She decided to go back to the pond.

The Great Doll Maker saw her plight and offered to restore her pretty face. The Great Doll Maker said that her new face might not be as beautiful as before.

Princess-Loves-the-Pond said, "That is alright. I want to *feel*, *see*, *hear*, *taste*, and *smell* the beauty of the world around me. I just want to love and be loved."

She was then no longer *The Beautiful Princess Without a Face*.

Sarah awoke from her daydream. She asked her mother, "Have you ever seen a doll without a face?"

Sarah's mother answered, "Grandma said sometimes dolls were made without a face to keep them from becoming vain."

"Now I know why that story was in my mind," Sarah breathed a sigh of relief. "I remember. Years ago, my Grandma told it to me."

Sarah held her new doll close to her body. She sweetly said, "I will always cherish you."

April Rachelle Robins - Author

The peaceful setting of her farm in the Red River Valley often inspires April Robins to paint her countryside in words. She is an honors graduate from Texas A&M University with a BS in Computer Science. After years of working on software projects related to the welfare of children, April retired and pursued her love of writing children's books. She is wife to Jay and mother-in-law to Celeste. She and Jay have four grandchildren.

F. Jay Robins – Co-Writer

Holding a degree in Aerospace Engineering from The University of Texas, Jay Robins worked in the aerospace industry for many years. Jay is an accomplished storyteller. He brings to the stories a creative mind and thought provoking insights.

Celeste Robins – Co-Writer

As a mother, homemaker, and an active school system volunteer, Celeste Robins' life is rich with purpose. Celeste has the uncanny ability to transpose any passage into a child's level of understanding.

Valerie Bouthyette – Illustrator

Every so often, an artistic talent comes along that catches your heart and your imagination. Valerie Bouthyette has that ability. She stirs memories of your childhood long forgotten and brings them to the forefront fresh and precious. For a moment, you become a kid again. Renowned for her broad graphic styles, Valerie was born on Long Island, New York. Today she lives on a farm in Pine City, New York, with her Canadian born husband, Pierre, and their dogs, Maggie and Amber. She is devoted to her children, Joseph and Katie, whose childhood inspires her creativity.

Printed in the United States
130998LV00002B